A Dog's
Night Before
Christmas

Sue Carabine

Illustrations by
Shauna Mooney Kawasaki

GIBBS·SMITH
P
PUBLISHER

SALT LAKE CITY

04 03   10 9

Copyright © 1996 Gibbs Smith, Publisher

Printed in China

Published by
Gibbs Smith, Publisher
P.O. Box 667
Layton, Utah 84041

ISBN 0-87905-762-9
ISBN 1-58685-125-X/GIFT

'Twas the night
before Christmas;
a huge storm
was brewing.

Santa looked out
to see what
the weather
was doing.

It made him
quite nervous—
though 'twas
Christmas Eve—

To take out the reindeer,
but he really must leave.

He bid all farewell
and went on his way,

Flying high
in the sky—
not a moment's delay.

Approaching a city,
he yelled,
"Ho! Ho! Ho!"

But the sleigh
hit a snowbank
as it came in so low.

Donner and Blitzen
knew something
was wrong;

The sleigh wouldn't move,
and Ol' St. Nick
was gone.

Comet then told them
he saw Santa sink

Way under the snow,
just as quick as a wink.

Cupid, the bright one,
said, "We must
get help

"From our friends
in this town
that bark, growl, and yelp.

There is *one* dog
who won't find
this job to be hard—

"The gentle and loving
but huge
St. Bernard."

They sent out the call
through the network
of hounds,

To please find a Saint
before morning
came 'round.

Shrudi the Sharpei
was licking
bones clean

When she got the message
and passed it to Dean.

Dean,
a long Dachshund,
was trying to think

Where he'd last seen
Bojangles—
perhaps at the shrink.

Bojangles the Saint
was really quite frisky,

But sometimes at Christmas
he was known to get tipsy!

Beatrice the Bassett
was seeing the vet

After trudging
through snow—
her long ears all wet.

Yes, she had seen Bo,
who was looking
quite hearty

After playing with kids
at the school
Christmas party.

When Lenny the Lab
heard the news
about Bo,

He was chasing
Miss Fifi
beneath mistletoe.

He rushed
to the door
and howled
at the moon,

And knew
if Bo heard him
he'd be there
real soon.

The howling of Lenny
rang out through
the night

Till the sweet
sounds of Christmas
went right out of sight!

Old English
could hear him
and howled along, too,

And his pal
Irish Wolfhound
made quite a to-do.

Very soon all the dogs,
both the pets
and the strays,

Were yelping and yapping
in all different ways.

The Cocker and Yorkshire
and spotted Dalmatian

Together with Setters
sent Bo's invitation

To please
return home
in a very great haste,

For Santa needs help
and there's
no time to waste.

Well, Bo got
the message and
lumbered on home—

His barrel was
bouncing, his mouth
dripped with foam.

Then he burrowed
his nose
way deep in the snow,

And he pulled
and he tugged
on Santa's big toe!

When St. Nick
popped out with
a sigh of relief,

The reindeer
and dogs heard
these words
from their chief:

"My friends
made the plea,
and you did not
fail them.

"May your New Year
be filled
with fire hydrants
and mailmen!"